BUSTER'S
first snow

By Hisako Madokoro   English text by Patricia Lantier   Illustrated by Ken Kuroi

**For a free color catalog describing Gareth Stevens' list of high-quality children's books,
call 1-800-341-3569 (USA) or 1-800-461-9120 (Canada).**

Library of Congress Cataloging-in-Publication Data

Madokoro, Hisako, 1938-
  [Yuki no hi no Korowan. English]
  Buster's first snow / text by Hisako Madokoro ;
illustrations by Ken Kuroi.
    p.   cm. — (The Adventures of Buster the puppy)
  Translation of: Yuki no hi no Korowan.
  Summary: Puppy friends Buster and Snapper find a
lost mitten in the snow and track down its owner.
  ISBN 0-8368-0492-9
  [1. Dogs—Fiction. 2. Snow—Fiction. 3. Lost and
found possessions—Fiction.] I. Kuroi, Ken, 1947- ill.
II. Title. III. Series: Madokoro, Hisako, 1938-
Korowan. English.
PZ7.M2657Bv   1991
[E]—dc20   90-47946

North American edition first published in 1991 by
Gareth Stevens Children's Books
1555 North RiverCenter Drive, Suite 201
Milwaukee, Wisconsin 53212, USA

This U.S. edition copyright © 1991. Text
copyright © 1991 by Gareth Stevens, Inc. First
published as *Yuki No Hi No Korowan* (*Korowan in
the Snow*) in Japan with an original copyright ©
1984 by Hisako Madokoro (text) and Ken Kuroi
(illustrations). English translation rights arranged
with CHILD HONSHA through Japan Foreign-
Rights Centre.

Gareth Stevens Children's Books
MILWAUKEE

Buster's footsteps crunched in the snow.

"Winter is very pretty!" he said as he looked at the white lawn.

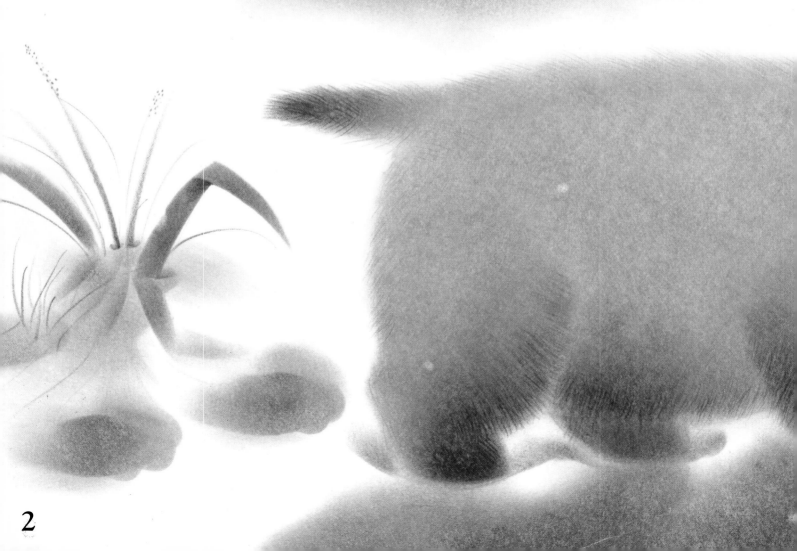

3

4

Buster saw somebody's footprints ahead of him in the snow. There was his best friend, Snapper!

"Let's play tag!"

5

The two puppies played
happily together. Suddenly,
a pile of snow fell right
onto their heads.

"Yikes! That's really cold!"
cried Buster and Snapper.

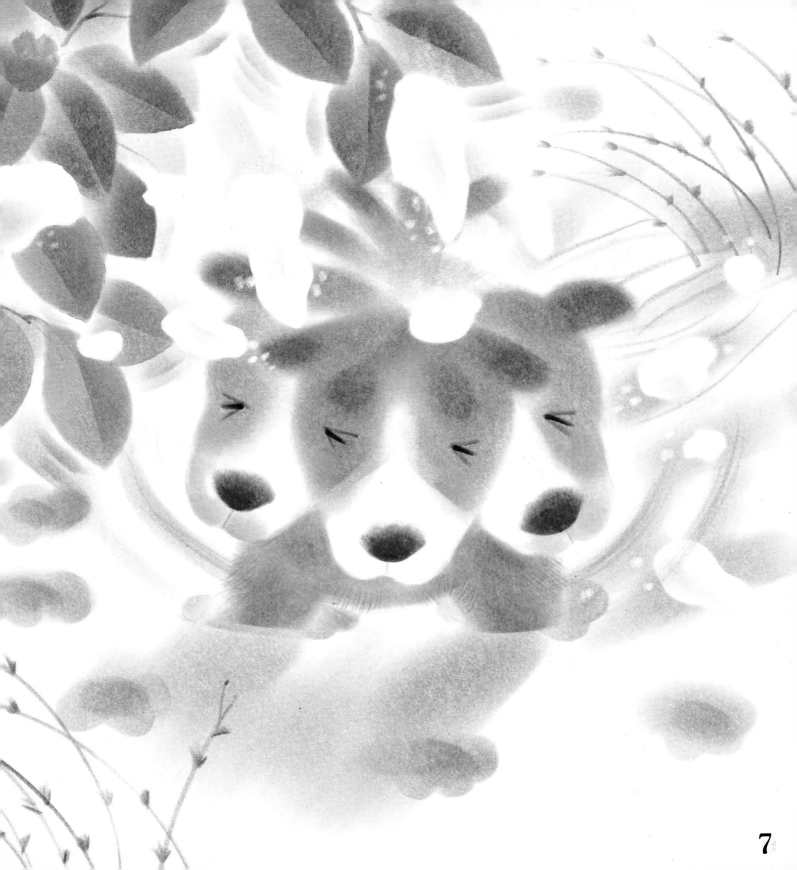

8

Buster looked up and
saw something strange in
the snow.

"Let's go dig it up!" he said.

9

Crunch. Crunch. Crunch.
The puppies found a
small glove.

"I wonder who it belongs to,"
said Snapper.

"Let's find the owner!" said
Buster. "We can follow the
footprints in the snow!"

14

Buster and Snapper soon saw a little girl wearing a cap. It had the same colors as the glove.

"She must be the owner!" said Snapper.

"Wait!" said Buster. "This girl
already has two gloves!"

17

The puppies followed
another set of icy footprints.

"Let's hurry!" said Buster.
"Someone's hand is getting
very cold!"

19

Buster and Snapper saw
many children playing in
the snow. One little girl
seemed to be looking for
something on the ground.

"There she is!" cried Buster.

20

21

"You found my glove!" said
the little girl. "My hand was
so very cold!"

She smiled happily at Buster
and Snapper.

The little girl asked the
puppies to play with her in
the park.

Buster was very happy.
He had made a new friend!